THE BRUJOS OF BORDERLAND HIGH
GUME LAUREL III
AF531037
WEST 44 BOOKS™

**Please visit our website, www.west44books.com.
For a free color catalog of all our high-quality books, call toll free 1-800-398-2504.**

Cataloging-in-Publication Data

Names: Laurel, Gume.
Title: The brujos of borderland high / Gume Laurel III.
Description: Buffalo, NY : West 44, 2025. | Series: West 44 YA verse
Identifiers: ISBN 9781978597365 (pbk.) | ISBN 9781978597358 (library bound) | ISBN 9781978597372 (ebook)
Subjects: LCSH: Witchcraft--Juvenile fiction. | Love--Juvenile fiction. | Magic--Juvenile fiction. | Gay teenagers–Juvenile fiction. | High school--Juvenile fiction.
Classification: LCC PZ7.1.L387 Br 2025 | DDC [F]--dc23

First Edition

Published in 2025 by
Enslow Publishing LLC
2544 Clinton Street
Buffalo, New York 14224

Editor: Caitie McAneney
Designer: Tanya Dellaccio Keeney

Photo Credits: Cover (clock) Tartila/Shutterstock.com; cover (snake) Updesign96/Shutterstock.com; cover (tarot card) Fer Gregory/Shutterstock.com.

Printed in the United States of America

CPSIA compliance information: Batch #CS25W44: For further information contact Enslow Publishing LLC at 1-800-398-2504.

For everyone who feels stuck in the past.
Ahead of you is a future filled with magic.

GLOSSARY

(in alphabetical order)

brujería: witchcraft; magical ability

brujos: male witches

chicharra: cicada

chismoso: gossiper

chupacabras: bloodsucking creatures

colcha: quilt

curandera: a female healing witch

Edgar haircut: Mexican American hairstyle

güero: light-skinned

lechuzas: female witches that morph into barn owls

Llorona: a Mexican ghost known for roaming near bodies of water

mijo: son

monitos: cartoons

neta: for real

ojo: evil eye

raspa: shaved ice

"Sana, sana, colita de rana": a Latin American verse for healing children

sirenas: female mermaids

takuache mullet: Mexican American hairstyle

tío: uncle

torta: a Mexican sandwich

Xolos (Xoloitzcuintli): Mexican hairless dogs; regarded by Indigenous groups as guardians, protectors, and guides for the soul on its journey to the underworld

zarape: Mexican poncho

OUR THREE-MONTH ANNIVERSARY

Gustavo drove us to watch
my favorite local band play.
At a high school house party
thrown by the popular seniors.

Glittery disco ball dots
on Gustavo's *güero* cheeks.
Like dancing freckles.
Our song pouring
from the speakers.
Like a waterfall
over our heads.
His warm body rocking mine.
Side to side.

Brujos.
Lechuzas.
Sirenas.
Chupacabras.

We were only two out of
dozens of magical creatures there.
But that moment in Gustavo's arms.
It made me feel like the house was
empty of any magic
except for our love.

He dumped me the following week.
After I caught him cheating
with some freshman.

THE FIRST CUT IS THE DEEPEST

Or so they say.

And maybe
they're not
totally wrong
about that.

Still.

Why would any
sane person put
themselves
at risk

to know
it hurts less
the second time?

I'VE LEARNED MY LESSON

I will never
love again.

Even if it means
no more
"Good Morning!"
text messages.
Or being shown
memes and told,
"This is so you!"

I'd rather stay

me,

myself,

and I.

Whatever it takes
to avoid another
heartbreak.
One even a
master *curandera*
can't heal.

BORDERLAND HIGH

Home of the Mighty Fighting *Xolos*!

Lockers. Desks.
Pencils. Textbooks.
Library. Band hall.
Gym. Football stadium.

A typical public high school
in the Lone Star State.
Where every student
is a magical creature.

Required classes:
Language Arts
Geometry
Alchemy
Ethics of Magic

And electives:
Animorphic Studies
Healing Work
Protection Spells
You and Your Magical Self

My favorite
class of all
is band.
That's where
my love
for piano
rings loudest.

MY *BRUJERÍA* IS SEEING THE PAST

I shuffle my
deck of cards.
Each one is
solid white,
with my initials
engraved in
rose gold.
A.Z. for Alejandro Zamora.

One by one,
I set down three. Left to right.
In the order that I lay them,
images appear in the cards.

A cracked mirror.
A snake swallowing its tail.
A broken clock.

Whenever I give someone
a card reading, the cards
always show a unique image.

Ever since Gustavo
broke my heart,
when I pull cards
for myself,
it reveals to me
these same

three images.

ZANDER APPROACHES

"Can I get a card reading?"
Zander asks me during our lunch period.
"I know you hate
being bugged for
readings at school.
But I can't remember
where I left my homework.
I thought maybe
you'd be able
to see where
I last left it."

"I hate being
bugged, in general."
I sip water from
my metal canteen.
It's covered in stickers.

"I'll give you a card reading
if you help me,"
Zander offers.
He brushes back his
black *takuache* mullet.

"I'll pass,"
I tell him.

ZANDER'S *BRUJERÍA* IS SEEING THE FUTURE

"The Winter Band Concert
is this weekend.
Don't you want to know
how many notes you'll miss?"
Zander sticks his tongue out.

I give him side-eye.

Zander gives me
puppy-dog eyes.
"Ale, please!"

Zander pulls out
a fruit cup
from his backpack.

Tart pineapple.
Juicy grapes.
Blue gelatin.

He holds it out to me.
Along with a spork.

I shrug my shoulders.
Swipe them
from his hand.

Zander slides
into the seat
ahead of me.

ONE-CARD PULL

An image
appears in
my card.

Zander slaps his forehead.
"Of course! I forgot to
check my band hall locker!"

I don't react to
his response.
I simply swallow
a spork-ful
of the fruit cup.

Then, I shuffle the card
back into my deck.

Zander pulls out
his deck of cards.
They're exactly like mine.
And exactly
like every other
brujo's deck of cards.
His initials are
engraved in emerald.

Z.A. for Zander Avaloz.

"Bruh, for real," I say.
"I don't care to know
anything about my future."

ZANDER SHUFFLES HIS CARDS

My head turns away.
To a random direction.
I instantly regret it.

Gustavo is walking
into the crowded cafeteria.
His arm is wrapped around
Rey's scrawny neck.

The guy he left me for.

My hands quickly brush my
bushy brown hair into place.
It was an Edgar haircut two
months ago. Now it's more
like an untamed mushroom.

Zander sees who
I'm scowling at.
He groans,
"It's been months already.
You still that bitter about it?"

I roll my eyes.
Look back at Zander.
Our espresso-brown eyes lock.

Zander says,
"Gustavo's *brujería* is
weaker than his bench press.
You're a thousand times
the *brujo* he'll ever be."

I snap,
"He's half *brujo*,
half vampire.
That makes *brujería*
harder for him than us."

"Ale, are you really
defending him right now?"

"Zander, shut up
and read my cards."

THREE-CARD PULL

A cracked mirror.

A snake swallowing its tail.

A broken clock.

I sigh.
"So, nothing new."

Zander asks,
"What do you mean?"

"That's the same
reading I get when
I pull cards for myself."

"Your past and future
look the same?"

"That's what
it looks like."

"That can't be good."

ZANDER IS A NICE GUY

He asks,
"Ale, is there anything
I can do to help?"

"There's nothing
to help with, Zander."
I stack my trash onto my
lunch tray. Even though
I haven't finished my meal.
"It is what it is."

"It doesn't have to
be, though. The ability
to know the future means
that we can learn what to
adjust in our present day.
That way, we can have
a better future."

"Well, my *brujería*
is seeing the past.
It looks like that's
where I'm meant to stay."

ZANDER SAYS SOMETHING

Likely something
he once read
in a Hallmark card.
I don't hear
exactly what.
I'm not
listening
anymore.

My attention
is on Gustavo.
He's running
his fingers
through his
boy toy's
straight hair.
Same way he
used to do
to me.

"Ale . . ." is the last
I hear of Zander
while rushing

out of

the

cafeteria.

MRS. DE LUNA'S ART CLASS

I enter the seemingly
empty art classroom.
Behind me, the heavy
metal door clinks shut.

Gentle hooting comes
from the steel rafters.
High above.

I respond,
"Hi, Mrs. De Luna."

My art teacher
comes gliding down.
Like a cloud.
In her *lechuza* form.
A white barn owl.
She lands behind me.

When I turn
in her direction,
she's back in
her human form.

"You're here early,"
Mrs. De Luna shakes
her long black hair.
White down feathers
fall out.

I say,
"Wanted to get a
jump start on my project."

She pauses.
Focuses on my eyes.
They're red. Puffy.
From crying in a
restroom stall
before coming
to her classroom.

My face darts
to the floor.

She asks,
"*Mijo*, are you okay?"

"It's . . .
Honestly . . .
It's nothing.
Promise.
I don't
want to
talk about it."

SEVENTH PERIOD ENDS

We all
pack up.

Mrs. De Luna tells us,
"Don't forget,
your self-portraits
are due next Monday.
That gives you
a whole week.
It's your last
assignment
before winter
vacation!"

I'm last
to reach
the exit.

"Ale,"
Mrs. De Luna calls.

I dread the
thought of her
asking about
earlier.

I TAKE A DEEP BREATH

Approach
Mrs. De Luna's
desk.

"Almost forgot.
I found this yesterday."
She holds out a *brujo* card.
"You must've dropped it."

I say,
"Can't be
one of mine.
All forty of mine
are accounted for.
I count them
several times a day."

"It's yours, Ale."
She hands it to me.

My rose gold initials
are on the card.

EIGHTH PERIOD

I count my
card deck.
Over and over.

I count 40.
Plus the one
Mrs. De Luna found.

That's 41 in total.

There's no denying
this card belongs to
my deck.

But it
makes
no sense.

Decks can
never have
more than
forty cards in total.
If a *brujo* ever
loses a card,
the card can
never be replaced.

I have no clue where
card 41
came from.

I STAY UP LATE

Bundled up in bed.
Surrounded by walls
covered in posters of
the coolest musicians.
Printed-out memes.
LED lights, too.

Dirty laundry
piled on the
desk chair.
And the desk.
And the floor.

I stare at my
deck of 40 cards.
They're neatly stacked
on my bedside
nightstand.

Beside them,
card 41.

I sense
in my heart
that I am
connected to it.

Yet,

my guts twist
into a pretzel
at the sight of it.

WHEN I CAN'T FALL ASLEEP

I do
what I
always do.

I scroll through
my old text
messages with
Gustavo.

Back when we
used to always text.
Before he blocked
my number.

WHEN WE FIRST STARTED TEXTING

Me

It's not even that funny.

Gustavo

what?! it's literally the funniest meme i've seen in my life.

Me

You have the worst taste in humor ever.

Gustavo

ur the one obsessed with that sylvanian *monitos* account.

Me

You don't understand art!!!

Gustavo

riiiight.

I TURN OVER IN BED

My eyes
catch sight
of a shadow.

Pouring into
my bedroom

from my open
window.

A man's silhouette!

Watching me!

SPINNING LIKE A TORNADO

I turn

to face

the window.

Nobody's there.

THE NEIGHBOR'S PIT BULL STARTS BARKING

I peek out
the window.

Scan the
overgrown
backyard
for movement.

Blurry, gray shadows.

Moonlight filtered
by thin clouds.

Everything is still.
Like a painting.

I shine my
phone's flashlight
for a clearer look.

Nothing.

Then,

the yellow
motion-sensitive
porch lights
flicker

on.

ALL I SEE IS A SHADOW

race over

the tall grass.

Jump the

wooden fence.

Escape into

the alley.

I couldn't see

their face.

DAD CALLS THE POLICE

The police show up
to check things out.

One sits with us
to go over details
on our dingy, beige
living room couches.
With mismatched
green pillows
older than me.

> "Lots of strange reports tonight,"
> says the officer.

"You think you'll find
the guy responsible?"
Tío Jorge,
who I call Dad,
asks him.

> "No telling,"
> the officer says.

"That's not comforting."
I cross my arms.

> "Our top unit of *lechuzas* are
> patrolling from the sky tonight,"
> the officer says.
> "If the culprit is out there,
> they'll find him."

IT'S 2 A.M.

How am I

supposed to

fall asleep

after all that?!

ONE MONTH INTO OUR RELATIONSHIP

Gustavo

ugh. yes. i love you. y u asking me again?

Me

I just like to hear it.

Gustavo

chill, bruh, lol.

Me

I already told you.
I hate it when you call me that.

I'm not your bruh!

Gustavo

lol.

Me

I'm not even joking!

Gustavo

cool story, bruh.

Me

Babe!!!

Gustavo

you love it, lol.

TRUTH IS

When he
pushed my
buttons like that,

I hated it.

More than
raspa brain freeze.

At the same time,
I loved
the rush
it gave me.

When he
treated me
that way.

No roller coaster
could compare.

HOMEWORK FOR LANGUAGE ARTS

I forgot to finish it.

I tell Mrs. Moody
about last night.

She says,
"It's okay, Ale.
I'm just glad
you're safe.
Bring me your
homework
tomorrow.
I won't
take away
any points."

A BIG QUESTION

What do you want to be
when you grow up?

No clue.

But that's the
homework assignment:

a letter
to Mrs. Moody
telling her all about it.

I ENJOY MARCHING BAND SEASON

That's when
I get to
play the
mellophone.

Being on
the field
all those
hours
darkens
my skin.
Like cedar.

For the
rest of the
school year,
we're indoors.
I revert back
to sandy tan.

That's when
I play the piano
for concert band.
My favorite
instrument.

This coming
Saturday night
is our
Winter Band Concert.

BAND IS THIRD PERIOD

We all take
our seats
before the
tardy bell rings.

I find my place
at the mahogany
baby grand piano.

Laid atop
the piano is a
giant black
leather folder.
It has all the
sheet music for
this school's
piano players.
As far back as
53 years.

I open it up.

An unexpected

surprise falls out.

Lands on my lap.

AN ORIGAMI PENGUIN

My favorite animal.
Folded from
rose gold
foil.

I look up.
Scan the
rest of the band.

Perhaps the person
who left this for me
is watching for
my reaction.

I HATE MYSELF FOR IT

but I look to the
drummers first.
Gustavo is thumbing
away at his phone.
Oblivious of the fact
that I'm even
in the room.

Flute section . . .
all are chattering.
Like parakeets.

Trombone section . . .
all are laughing.
Over a dirty joke.

Clarinet section . . .
all are tuning
their instruments,

except for Zander.

ZANDER'S LOOKING MY WAY

With eyes wider
than Texas highways.

He points at me

and shouts,

"Behind you!"

THE BAND KIDS SCRAMBLE

Everyone screams.
Like ghouls.
Like this is a concert
mixed with the
jump scare of a
horror movie.

I look
behind me.

I start
screaming, too.

A *CHICHARRA* THE SIZE OF A BULL

It's peeking into
the band hall.
Through the
open doorway
behind me.

A green and white
exoskeleton.
Six long,
hairy legs.
Wings.
Like stained
glass windows.
Colored turquoise
and clear.

The *chicharra* rattles.
Louder than
all our screams
combined.

IT CREEPS INTO THE BAND HALL

It swings its head
back and forth.
Like an axe.
Flinging music stands
and chairs across the room.

It flaps its wings.
Faster than the
speed of gossip spreading.
All the loose sheet music
in the room spirals
into a tornado.

Before I can move,
it charges toward me.

IT SWINGS ITS HEAD AT ME

I throw myself
to the ground.
Narrowly dodge it.

The *chicharra*
bashes its head
into the piano.

An explosion!

Shards of wood and ivory
fly

everywhere.

Like

candy

from

a

piñata.

THE *CHICHARRA* STANDS OVER ME

I stare into
its five eyes.
Each of them
holds a clear
reflection
of me
trembling.

Scared.

Alone.

Frozen.

The *chicharra*
rattles even louder.
Opens its mouth.

Prepares to eat me
in one gulp.

DIRECTOR TO THE RESCUE

Band Director Guerrero calls out,
"Away from him!"

A bolt of
purple lightning
crashes through
the air.

Pierces one of the
chicharra's eyes.
Like a sword.

The *chicharra's*
eye cracks.
Like a mirror.

I know that
purple lightning.

It comes from
Director Guerrero's wand.
The one she uses
to conduct
the band with.

BEFORE I CAN MOVE

the *chicharra* screeches.
Horribly loud.
My eardrums swell.
Like balloons
ready to pop
from too much air.

The *chicharra* turns.
Faces Director Guerrero.

As it does,
one of its
swinging
legs swats me.
Like a metal bat
to a baseball.

I'm sent

soaring

across

the

band hall.

ZANDER TRIED TO CATCH ME

Rather, he says
that's how he
ended up with
a bloody nose.

I blacked out
from the fall.
The last thing
I remember
is being flung
through the air.

I eventually
woke up.

On a cot
in the
school
curandera's
office.

I GROAN AND SIT UP

"You feeling better yet, Mr. Alejandro?"
asks Señora Mendez,
the school *curandera.*
"Or should I recite another
'Sana, sana, colita de rana'?"

"No. I'm fine."
I stretch my back.

"You're not fine, Ale,"
says Zander.
He's at my bedside.

"You worry too much, bro."
When I say this,
the bottom of my chin stings.
Like 20 wasps attacked it.

I touch my chin.

It's covered with
gauze and bandages.

ZANDER EXPLAINS

"A music stand to the jaw
during the fall,"
Zander says.
"You were a
little less
falling star.
A little more
Humpty-Dumpty."

"I healed it up
best I could,"
Señora Mendez
walks over.
She inspects
her handiwork.
"It'll sting for
another hour or two.
Definitely gonna
leave a scar.
But my *brujería*
sealed it up tight.
No need for stitches.
You can remove the
bandage if you'd like."

OUCH!

I rip off the bandage
in one swoop.
My eyes water.
Like teacups
filled to the brim.

"Scar's not so bad, actually,"
Zander takes a
photo of it with
his phone.
He shows me
the photo.

A dark-violet,
upside-down arch.
On the right side of
my jawline.

Zander says,
"If we add some
googly eyes,
it'll look like a
smiley face."

I shoot him the
meanest side-eye
possible.

DAD ISN'T ANSWERING

Señora Mendez says,
"I haven't been able to
get ahold of your father
yet, Mr. Alejandro."

I say,
"He can't take calls
while on the clock.
His boss at the
car garage is a jerk."

Señora Mendez asks me,
"Is there anyone else
we can call?"

I hate this question
more than any other
question adults ask me.
When you have only
one parent,
you get asked that
question too often.
Especially when
you don't have
birth parents
for a reason
like mine.

"No,"
I answer
Señora Mendez.
"I'm fine. Really."

DURING DAD'S LUNCH BREAK

He listens to
the 10 voicemails
Señora Mendez sent him.

Dad speeds to
Borderland High.
Has me pulled out
of fifth-period history.

"Nah, nah,"
Dad disagrees
when I tell him
I'm fine.
"I'm taking you
home for the day."

IN DAD'S PICKUP

We make
our way through
the school parking lot.

City and school officers
are gathered in the grass.
Around the charred remains
of the *chicharra*.

Director Guerrero
left it smoking.
Like a hunk of brisket.

I wish she had
burned it to ash.

That monster
destroyed the
school's only

piano.

One of my
few sources
of peace.

MY ANCIENT ELECTRIC PIANO DOESN'T CUT IT

My thumb
presses down
the middle C note.
The white plastic key
creaks from old age.
The wobbly
electronic sound
is off pitch.

Even if it were
brand-new,
it would still be
too small
to play
double octaves
with my left hand.

DAD SHOUTS ON THE PHONE

I hear him clearly.
Even with my
bedroom door
closed.

"No, Sanchez!
I can't go back in today!
I'm not leaving him here alone!
. . . Yes! A giant *chicharra*!
. . . No! I've never heard of
such a thing before either!
. . . Alright! Alright. Thanks.
Yes. Tomorrow. I'll be there."

DAD ALWAYS KNOCKS FIRST

"It's open,"
I call out,
seated at
my electric piano.

Dad opens the door and says,
"Sorry about all that."

Dad stretches his left leg
while walking up to me.
Softly moans as he does.

An old injury
we never talk about.
Always hurts most when
it's getting cold out.

He asks,
"You okay, Ale?"

"Dad.
I told you.
I'm fine."

"Ain't no way
I believe that."

I groan,
"I swear.
I'm fine.
The school *curandera*
fixed me up.
No broken bones
or nothing."

"She can't fix
what's in here,"
Dad's calloused
finger taps my chest.
"You've had two
scary encounters.
Back-to-back!
Like someone
gave you *ojo*
or something.
It's okay
to not feel okay."

I haven't
felt okay
in a long time.

WE PICK UP TACO P. FOR DINNER

Over the drive-through speaker,
the cashier says,
"I'll have your total
at the window!"

There are
three cars
ahead of us.

Classic rock
plays on the radio.
Dad and I sit silent.
Staring at our phones.

Dad's phone dings.

My eyes
sneakily drift
from my phone screen

          to his.

Dad's chatting
with a match
on a dating app.

CHISMOSO

I say,
"Didn't know
you were into
vampires."

"*Chismoso*!"
Dad shuts his
phone screen off.

I say,
"She's cute.
Have y'all met yet?"

Dad says,
"Not like I have
time to date."

"You should
make time to date."

"And what
about you, Ale?"

"What *about*
me, Dad?"

Dad's eyebrows lift.
"You dating anyone?"

I WISH I COULD ESCAPE THE PICKUP

I nearly puke,
"Daaaddddd . . ."

"I'm only asking, Ale.
That's what
caring parents do, right?
They ask questions."

"No."

"No to what?"

"No
to
all
of
the
above."

"Ale."

WE REACH THE DRIVE-THROUGH WINDOW

My body
locks up
when I see
the cashier.

It's Rey.

Gustavo's . . . *boyfriend*.

Rey tells Dad,
"That'll be $19.86, please."

Before Rey notices me,
I turn away.
Make sure he can't
see my face.

"Green or red salsa?"
Dad asks me.

"Green . . ."
I whisper.

"Speak up, son . . ."

"Green . . ."
I whisper
one decibel
louder.

"Al—"

"Green,"
I cough.
Loud enough
for Dad to hear.
Before he says
my name
in front
of Rey.

BACK AT HOME

Dad says,
"You can stay home
from school tomorrow
if you want."

He takes a bite of
his beef fajita taco.

I wash my hands
in the kitchen sink.
"Nah. I have an important
assignment due tomorrow.
Can't miss turning it in."

"That can't actually
be what you want,"
Dad wipes his
greasy hands
on his jeans.
Reaches into
his back pocket.
Pulls out
his deck of
brujo cards.

DAD'S *BRUJERÍA*

is seeing what you
desire most.

I say,
"Dad. You know
I don't like
you doing
brujería
on me."

"My *brujería* is
every parent's dream.
It'd be a crime to not
use it on my teenage son!"
Dad laughs.

I roll my eyes.

Dad pulls out
a single card
from his deck.

He asks it,
"Does Ale want to go to
school tomorrow or not?"

I fake laugh.
Take off to my bedroom.
Don't bother to see
what the card shows him.

WHAT DO I WANT TO BE WHEN I GROW UP?

This blank sheet
of lined paper
is a time portal.
Into the multiverse of
all my possible futures.

Ones in which I grow up to be:

> A famous sandcastle builder
> on the beaches of Ibiza.
>
> An undercover private investigator
> running the mean streets of NYC.
>
> The person who gets paid to say,
> "This call cannot be completed as dialed."

Since these possibilities
are make-believe,

I'd also like to be
happy when I grow up.

THIS BLANK SHEET

of lined paper
becomes
a black hole.

All my insecurities

fall

into

it.

I always feel like
everyone knows
something I don't.

Whatever that
something is,
it's what helps them
be normal.

How to
walk.
Talk.
Dress.
Exist.
Like it's all natural.

I want to be someone

who fits in.

I always feel like
everyone knows
something I don't.

Whatever that
something is,
it's what helps them
hang in there.

No matter the setback.
Their eyes stay on the prize.

I want to be someone

who moves forward.

I always feel like
everyone knows
something I don't.

Whatever that
something is,
it's what helps them
feel loved.

Fully.
Not like
they owe
anyone
anything
for it.

I want to be someone

who is healed.

Dear Mrs. Moody,

The summer before sixth grade,
my dad took me to Port Aransas.
There were countless seashells that
had washed up onto the dry, sandy shore.
None of those shells intended to end up
baking in the sand. Bleached of their bright
colors and special patterns. Stepped on.
Chipped. Pocketed by tourists. You think that's
the future they imagined for themselves?
Back home in the salt water? No. They didn't see
that coming. They were forced to go whichever way
the waves decided to send them.

I am a shell. So are you. So is everyone else.
I didn't choose to have a heart that always feels
everything loudly. To have a *brujería* that keeps
me focused on the past.

The waves of life rocked me the ways they have.
Without my input.
You're asking me what I want to be?
I can't give you an answer.
I don't want to be let down
when life doesn't happen
the way I'm hoping it will. I think
doing that in the past is what has
given me this gloomy outlook on the future.

Magically,

A.Z.

PS: Please don't show this to the guidance counselor.

THE NIGHT I CAUGHT GUSTAVO CHEATING

Me

Please text me back, babe.

Please. Don't ignore me.

Why would you do this to me?

I love you so much.

Please answer.

WEDNESDAY BAND CLASS

The baby grand piano
is now a pile of rubble.
Brushed into a corner
of the band hall.

I stand over it.
It looks how I feel.

Something shimmers
within the rubble.
I reach for it.
Pull out the
crumpled remains
of the rose gold
origami penguin.

I still don't know
who made it.

"You alright?"
Zander walks up to me.
"You haven't responded
to any of my texts."

"Sorry. I haven't
checked my phone,"
I lie.

I toss the origami penguin
back into the rubble.

NO PIANO FOR ME

"We'll try to have one
ready at the auditorium
in time for this weekend's concert,"
Director Guerrero assures me.
"Until then,
you'll have to
practice at home."

ZANDER STOPS ME AFTER SCHOOL

"You must've dropped this earlier."
Zander hands me a brujo card.
It has my initials in rose gold.

"Something isn't right,"
I pull my deck of 40 cards
out of my back right pocket.
"See this? It's all forty."

I pull out the card
Mrs. De Luna found
from my back left pocket.
"This is a forty-first card that
was found the other day.
But it doesn't belong to me.
Now, you've found a
forty-second card."

Zander scrunches
his eyebrows.
"These couldn't belong
to anyone else."

I say,
"Exactly why none
of this makes sense."

"Have you tried
using your cards?
To see if they show you
the past of these other cards?
Like where they came from?"

"I've already told you.
When I pull cards for myself,
they show me nothing except
the same three images."

A cracked mirror.

A snake swallowing its tail.

A broken clock.

ZANDER AND I ENTER MY HOUSE

Zander goes into the bathroom.
Dad whispers to me,
"Ale, you know I don't
like company over
without you asking
permission first."

"I wasn't expecting you
to be home so early."
I shrug my shoulders.

Dad's caterpillar eyebrows
rise up to his buzz cut.

"Not . . . not that we were . . . "
I scramble for words.
"We weren't up to
anything like that . . ."

Zander walks back into the kitchen.
Wipes his hands dry
against his evergreen hoodie.

"We'll be in my room, Dad,"
I say.

Dad stretches
a hand out
and says,
"Ale, wait . . ."

DAD'S BESTIE, BRISA

suddenly walks into the kitchen.
Carrying her pink toolbox.

When she sees me,
her eyes widen.
To the size of
basketballs.

"Shoot!"
Brisa freezes in place.

"Am I Medusa-ing
you or something?"
I joke.

"You said he wouldn't
be here this early,"
Brisa murmurs to Dad.

My hands rest on my hips.
"Dad, what's going on?"

SURPRISE!

"Wanted it to be a surprise."
Dad walks me, Zander, and Brisa
into my bedroom.
"Either way, I think
you'll be happy."

My old, crummy
electric piano is gone.
In its place is a new one.
State of the art. Polished.
With 88 keys. Weighted.
A stand that makes it look like
an actual upright piano.

"Arrived at the shop yesterday!"
Brisa squeezes my shoulders.
"Fresh out of the box.
Not one soul has played it yet."

"Go ahead, Ale,"
Dad slides out the new
matching piano stool.
"Give it a try."

I sit on the jet-black,
cushioned bench.
It's so stiff and new.
It doesn't make even
the tiniest creak.

With a push of the ON button,
the piano comes alive.
The screen lights up
like the night sky.

My eyes fill with stars.

SOUND 0001: GRAND PIANO

My right foot hovers
over the gold pedals.
I carefully push down
on each one.

My fingertips
graze the keys.
Like feathers.
I can tell how
heavy each key is.

I'm scared to play

my first note.

If I play a first note,
then that means
there'll be a last note.

Maybe not today.
Or tomorrow.
Or next year.

But one day.

Then, all I'll have
are memories.
Memories
overpowered
by the silence

I'm left to sit with.

ZANDER STANDS TO MY LEFT

He places his hand
on my shoulder.

"Don't act shy now,"
Zander whispers.

"I love it. Really,"
I tell Dad.
"I'm just nervous to play
in front of y'all, right now.
Especially before
I can test it out
in private."

"Better get over those nerves
before Saturday's concert."
Dad's smile weakens.
"There'll be a lot more
than three people watching
you onstage."

AFTER ZANDER AND BRISA LEAVE

"For real though.
Thanks, Dad,"
I say while he
rubs his aching leg.
"Owning a piano like that
is something I've never
even dreamed of."

"Remember how
I pulled a card
for you last night?"
Dad confesses.
"The card showed me
an image of you
playing the piano at school.
It's what you desired most.
So, I had to make sure you
had a good one on hand.
Especially now that you
don't have one at school."

LATER THAT NIGHT

I leave the
new piano

turned on.

Blue waves
of screen light
dance on my
popcorn ceiling.

Like aurora borealis.

Or sunlight
hitting pool water.

THE MORNING AFTER I CAUGHT GUSTAVO CHEATING

Gustavo

you're overreacting.
stop calling me over and over.

Me

Why won't you answer my call?

I just want to talk.

Gustavo

there's nothing to talk about.

we are done.

Me

No. Please. Stop saying that.
Please stop it, babe.

Can we at least talk?

Gustavo

leave me alone!

i don't want to talk to you!

go away!

THIS MORNING

Dad cooks scrambled eggs and weenies.
Crackling grease.
Metal spatula scraping pan.
Morning news on the television
streaming from the living room.

"Ran out of tortillas,"
Dad tells me when I enter the kitchen.
"Gonna have to eat these with a fork."

"Cool." I take a seat on a barstool.
Since we don't have a dining table.
Fold my arms over the kitchen bar ledge.
Bury my face in my arms.

Dad asks, "You not sleep well?"

"There's never enough hours to sleep well."
I force myself to sit up.

Dad steps away from the stove.
Raises an eyebrow as he thumbs my chin.
Like he's wiping off dried saliva.
"That school *curandera*
did a good job patching you up.
No scab or nothing. Just a straight up scar."
Dad returns to the stove.

Great. Another scar to add to my list.
At least it's not another open wound.

DAD HANDS ME A STEAMING PLATE

Before I take a bite,
the morning news
makes our heads turn.

The news anchor says,
"Sometime last night,
a fire broke out at the
Borderland High School auditorium."

Dad and I rush up to the television.
I grab the remote.
Raise it to max volume.

The news anchor continues,
"There are no victims
or reported injuries.
Auditorium security footage
recorded the moments
leading up to the fire."

GRAINY SECURITY FOOTAGE

It shows the dark lobby
entrance of the auditorium.
A hooded figure approaches
one of the glass double-door entrances.
He's shuffling a deck of cards.
Like a poker dealer in Las Vegas.

A *brujo*.

He touches one card
to the glass double door.
Ice spreads across the glass.
Like a spider weaving its web.

Once the door is frozen solid,
the *brujo* bashes his shoulder into it.
The door shatters into countless pieces.
Without causing any harm to the *brujo*.

"Cold Magic?"
I ask aloud.

Dad says nothing back.
His flaring nostrils say it all.

Next, the *brujo*
enters the lobby.
Without a care for
being seen or caught.

He walks directly
beneath the security camera.

His hood shields
most of his face.
But the scar
on his chin
is clearly visible.

It's identical to mine.

DAD QUICKLY LOOKS MY WAY

Squints at my scar.

"I was home all last night,"
I say before he
accuses me of anything.
"I don't ever sneak out. I swear."

"Cold Mag—"
Dad starts to shout,
but stops himself.
He can't even say it.

I say,
"I would never."
My chest becomes heavy.
"I swear it.
I swear on my deck.
I would never."

Dad takes deep breaths.
Blinks furiously.
Grunts and grips
his aching leg.

We look back
to the television.

THE SECURITY FOOTAGE SHOWS THE EMPTY LOBBY

The *brujo* is out of sight.
Likely in the auditorium.

Seconds later,
he returns to the lobby.
Carrying two
bass drum mallets.
Their poofy ends
engulfed in flames.

He spins them.
Like color guard batons.
While doing this, he dances.

Spins.
Jumps.
Kicks.

Some sort of ritual.

Until the fire
changes color.

From orange

to blue.

THE *BRUJO* KEEPS DANCING

From one corner
of the lobby
to the other.

He touches
the fiery mallets
to anything that
might catch fire.

Stacks of fliers
for upcoming events.
Posters.
Banners.
Wooden chairs.
Couches filled with
cheap cushioning.

Within moments,
the lobby
becomes a firepit.

The security footage

goes

offline.

ON THE DRIVE TO SCHOOL

Dad doesn't
say anything.

Each time my nerves
can't take the silence
any longer, I say,
"It wasn't me, Dad. I swear."

We pull into the
student drop-off area.
Dad shifts the gear

into park.

I say it one last time,
"It wasn't me."

Dad finally looks me in the face.
"I believe you, Ale.
I trust it wasn't you.
I know you're
smarter than that.
You of all people
know better than
to mess with
Cold Magic."

COLD MAGIC

It's why
I became
Tío Jorge's son
when I was
five years old.

It's why
Tío Jorge
became my dad
when he was
20 years old.

It's why
I don't have a
biological father
anymore.

HIS NAME WAS ÁNGEL

His name
might
still be
Ángel.

Nobody's sure
if he's even
alive or not.

It's been
that long
since anyone
heard about

him.

MOM DIED DURING THE PANDEMIC

Ángel became
obsessed with
bringing her back
from the dead.

Brujería that alters
the natural flow
of past timelines.
It's considered
Cold Magic.

Forbidden
across the world.
It's like a drug.
It consumes.
Devours.
Makes you a slave
to bitterness.
Anger.
Emotions
more chilling
than we have
words for.

Cold Magic
freezes
your heart
alive.

IT'S MY GREATEST FEAR

That the part of Ángel
that gave in to
Cold Magic

is sleeping

somewhere

inside of me.

I WALK INTO MRS. MOODY'S CLASS

Everyone quickly hushes.

Stares.

"It does look like it,"
Jason Orozco whispers.

"There's no way it wasn't him,"
Christabell Nuñez mumbles.

I ignore them.
As if I can't hear.
As if nothing is happening.

Over the intercom,
Principal Aguayo
greets the school.

MORNING ANNOUNCEMENTS

Principal Aguayo leads us
in the Pledge of Alliance.
It's our country's vow.
Honoring the belief
that all magical beings
should live in harmony.

Then, the Texas Pledge.
Because this is Texas
and that's simply
how we do things here.

She moves on to
upcoming events.
Lunch meal of the day.

Then, she says,
". . . And I'm sure you are
all wondering about
this Saturday's
Winter Band Concert."

I sit up in my seat.

Principal Aguayo says,
"Thanks to Borderland's
Llorona Fire Stoppers,
the blaze was put out
before spreading
beyond the lobby!"

Out of the corner of my eye,
I see students looking at me.
Whispering into
each other's ears.

Principal Aguayo says,
"The main auditorium
was untouched.
It is in perfect condition!
We will be holding the
Winter Band Concert,
as scheduled!"

The other band kids
in class cheer.

I sigh.

Relieved.

ENTERING THE BAND HALL

Everyone's watching me.
The way they did in
Mrs. Moody's class.

I spend the entire period sitting
in a metal folding chair
where the piano used to be.
Tapping my fingers on my thighs
while the band plays.
Rehearsing the piano part
in my head.

"Mr. Maldonado."
Director Guerrero calls on Gustavo.
"Put that phone away
before I take it away.
That's your final warning."

For the rest of band class,
Gustavo waits for
Director Guerrero
to look away.
When she does,
Gustavo busts out
his phone.
Grinds his teeth.
Texts fast.
Like it's a race.

LUNCHTIME

Zander texts me.
Asks where I am.
I tell him I'm
spending lunchtime
in the library.

I don't invite him.
But I know he'll
show up anyway.

Librarian Quilantán
spots me at a table
in the back corner
of the library.

She pushes a cart of books.
"*Mijo*! I haven't seen you in forever!"

I say,
"Don't worry, Miss. I'm still reading.
Just been too busy to come by."

She says,
"The library will always be here for you.
No matter what you have going on."

I nod.

"Here, check out this book
before you leave."
Librarian Quilantán hands
me a book from her cart.

I read the title aloud.
Emo Poems for Emo Brujos.
"Miss, I don't think I
consider myself emo."

She winks.
Walks off with her book cart.
"Have a good day, Alejandro."

ZANDER SHOWS UP

"Do people even
still say *emo*?"
Zander slides into
a chair at my table.

I'm already on the
book's ninth poem.

I set the book down.
"Today sucks."

Zander sticks his tongue out.
"Well, I guess some people
still live up to the name."

ZANDER STARES AT MY SCAR

"You, too?!"
I groan.

"Wait . . ."
Zander snaps out of it.
"No . . . I don't
believe the rumors."

"It's a rumor already?!"

"I mean,
the resemblance
is uncanny."

"Zander . . ."

"I know it wasn't you, Ale.
Who cares what everyone
has to say about it?"

"*Everyone*?!"
I sink into my chair.

"Besides, there are way
juicier rumors
going around today."

"Like what?"
My *chismoso*-self
leans forward.

"Surprised you haven't heard yet,"
Zander leans forward.
"Gustavo and Rey.
It's not looking good."

I gasp,
"He cheated on Rey?"

"Not sure on details.
But they're fighting.
And it's bad."

SUDDENLY

a chilling breeze
sweeps through
the library.
Like when you try to
blow out a
stubborn candle.

At first, gentle.
Then, forceful.

Flapping book pages.
Composition paper.
Like leaves in the air.

The angry breeze
becomes colder
by the second.

Everyone
grabs their
backpacks,
jackets,
and books.

Librarian Quilantán yells,
"Evacuate the library
in a safe and orderly manner!"

OF COURSE

this only causes
more panic.

Everyone rushes
for the exit.
Like rainwater
down a gutter drain.

ZANDER AND I RUN

"What's happening, Miss?!"
I shout to Librarian Quilantán.

"I'm not sure, Ale,"
she answers.
"You two
get out of
here. *Pronto*!"

Zander
and I
are the
last students
to reach

the exit.

Before we
touch the doors,
they turn to

solid ice.

I CAN SEE MY BREATH

Puffs of warm steam
meeting cold air.
Sheets of ice grow
over the walls. The floor.

We back away from the exit.
One foot at a time.

Nowhere to move.
We become trapped
where we stand.

The cold wind gathers
at the center of the library.

It becomes a

spinning tornado of

dark-blue smoke,

flakes of charcoal,

white grains of sand.

It spins faster.

And faster.

With every

passing second.

THE COLD AIR STINGS

Like mosquito bites.

I cross my arms
over my chest.

Zander stands
in front of me.
Turns his back
to the tornado.
Wraps his arms
around me.

I lean against him.
Bury my face
beneath his chin.

With one eye open,
I peek over
Zander's shoulder.

When the tornado
can spin no faster,

it implodes.

In place of
the tornado
now stands
a hooded man.

Tall.
Slender.

His long black robe
piles at his feet.
Like trees with
roots above the soil.

His face is hidden
by a mask
made of mirrors.

He looks around
the library and hisses,
"Where . . . is . . . he . . .?"

BATTLE IN THE LIBRARY

Librarian Quilantán shouts,
"You do not belong here!"
She and her library assistants
rush toward the hooded man.

Before reaching him,
they all hunch forward.
Dark green scales
grow over their skin.
Hands and feet
form into massive claws.
Eyes widen. Turn crimson red.
Long tails grow.
Spikes run down their backs.
Saliva drips from their fangs.

They've morphed
into their *chupacabra* forms.

They swat their claws and tails
at the hooded man.

His bony hands
in black gloves
block their attacks.
They can't get a single hit in.

One *chupacabra* whips
her tail at his face.

His mask is knocked off.
It shatters on the floor.

THE HOODED MAN PANICS

Tries to
hide his face
with his hands.

His skin
isn't human.

It's rattlesnake skin.

His eyes are
solid white.
Like snow.

A demon.

I notice
his chin.

A long
maroon
scar.

Like mine.

He sees me seeing him.

RATTLING FILLS THE AIR

Like pebbles
in a rain stick.
It comes from
every direction.
Followed by the

hiss of a snake.

My lungs
turn into
icebergs.

BEHIND ME

the frozen
exit doors
are smashed
to pieces.

School security officers
rush in.
Wands in hand.

"Get these kids
out of here!"
the commanding
officer orders.

An officer grabs
me and Zander.
Yanks us backward.

My eyes finally
break away from
the demon's eyes.

My vision gets fuzzy.

Dizzy.

Stumbling.

BATTLE'S END

All the officers
aim their wands
at the demon.

The librarian
chupacabras
duck for cover.

My lungs
force in a
gulp of air.

At this same moment,

I

lose

my

balance.

I'M FALLING

As I fall,
so does
the demon.

We hit the ground
at the same time.

Once the demon
touches the ground,
it disappears.

In a flash of
blue and white
lightning.

As if it were
never even
there.

All returns
to normal.

THURSDAY NIGHT

Dad and I watch
the nightly local news.

"A time-traveling demon!"
Dad repeats the
news anchor's words.
"I knew it!"

The news anchor continues,
"Authorities believe
it time traveled to our
current year and ended up
in the Borderland High library
without meaning to.
All signs show
the demon has returned
to its own time period.
Or, at the very least,
has left ours."

THE NEWS FOOTAGE CUTS

to a press conference.
Held by Principal Aguayo.

She says to the audience,
"To be safe,
Borderland High
will be closed tomorrow.
Classes will resume on Monday.
Now, I know our band students
have worked tirelessly
to prepare for Saturday's concert . . ."

I sit upright.

Principal Aguayo says,
"For that reason,
we have decided
to not cancel
the Winter Band Concert."

Dad jumps up.
"Are you serious?!"

Principal Aguayo assures that
there will be extra security
on site for it.

Dad turns the
television off.
"You're not going."

I JUMP OFF THE COUCH

"I have to go!"
I shout.

Dad throws his arms up.
"You almost got hurt, again!"

I say,
"Wrong place
at the wrong time!"

"No, Ale."

"Dad!
I've been practicing
for the concert for months!"

"It's too dangerous!"

"I'm the only
piano player!
There's no backup!"

"There'll be more concerts."

I SLAM MY BEDROOM DOOR

Grab my binder of
piano sheet music.
Throw it against the wall.
Pages fly everywhere.

Dad knocks loudly.

Shakes the doorknob.

Shouts my name.

"Leave me alone!"
I yell.

Dad starts pounding the door.
Yells even louder.

"Go away!"
I scream.

We go back and forth
for a few more minutes.

I throw myself on the bed.
Sob into my pillow.
Dad stomps off.
Slams his bedroom door shut.

For the rest of the night,
my bedroom is a cage.

THE LAST TIME ÁNGEL WAS AROUND

I'm wrapped
in a blanket.
Door closed.
Ears covered.
But I can still
hear them in
the living room.

Dad yells,
"You can't keep doing this, Ángel!"

Ángel yells back,
"I can't stop!"

"You need to!"

"It's not that simple!"

Boots scrape floor.
Panting. Walls shake.
Picture frames fall. Shattered glass.

Ángel yells,
"Let me go, Jorge!"

Dad yells,
"We need to get you help, Ángel!"

"No!"

Hissing. Rattling.
Furniture turned over.
Loud thud on the floor.

Ángel yells,
"Jorge! Get up!
I didn't mean to hurt you!
Jorge! Get up!"

Front door swings open.
Footsteps out the door.
Down the sidewalk.
Fading away.

DAYS AFTER I CAUGHT GUSTAVO CHEATING

Me

please. don't abandon me.

don't ghost me.

please.

A KNOCK

wakes me up Friday morning.

I stumble out of my bedroom.
Dad has answered the door.

"Really, you didn't have to,"
Dad says to a woman
standing on the front porch.

Caramel skin.
Straight black hair
down to her waist
Fire truck–red
leather jacket.
She's balancing
three coffee cups.

"It's no problem. Promise."
The woman smiles widely.
Her sharp fangs show.

She's the vampire
Dad matched with
on the dating app.

HER ACORN EYES SHIFT MY WAY

Dad realizes
I'm standing
behind him.

He clears his
throat to say,
"Ale . . .
this . . .
this is Nani.
My . . . friend."

MORNING COFFEE

Nani and I sit
at the kitchen bar.
Dad stands in front of us.

I take a sip of the coffee
Nani brought for me.
"Cinnamon?"
I ask.

"Just a pinch,"
she nods.
"A pinch of something sweet
can make a world of difference."

I take a longer sip.

Dad's phone rings.
He steps into the
living room to answer.

CHATTING WITH NANI

"Hear you're
pretty good
at piano,"
Nani says.

"Doesn't matter,"
I huff.
"Dad isn't letting me
play at my concert tomorrow."

"He's only looking
out for you.
It's a lot of responsibility,
you know.
Raising a teenage brujo."

"I wouldn't know."
I sip my coffee.

"Neither would I."
She sounds as if she's
thankful for not knowing.

This makes me grin.

Nani grins back.

DAD ARGUES OVER THE PHONE

He's talking
to his boss.
About how
he has to
stay home.

With me.

About how
he can't go
back to work
until Monday.

His boss
isn't happy
about it.

"It's not fair," I sigh.
"Always feeling like
everything's my fault."

Nani says,
"Would you
believe me
if I told you
it's not your fault?"

I take
another
long sip.

Nani whispers,
"I'm sure your dad feels
the same way you do.
For plenty of his own reasons.
Over stuff out of his control.
Same as you."

Dad ends
his call.

"Do me a favor, Alejandro.
Cut him a little slack.
I promise you.
He's doing his best."

Dad returns
to the kitchen.
Apologizes
for the uproar.

Nani and I say
we don't know
what he's talking about.

FOR THE REST OF FRIDAY

Dad and Nani
watch movies
in the living room.

I brainstorm ideas
for Mrs. De Luna's
self-portrait assignment.
It's due Monday.

I sketch samples
in my notebook.

None of them
feel right.

ZANDER ARRIVES BEFORE SUNSET

He found
a third card.
One that belongs
to my deck.
But isn't one
of my 40 cards.

I gasp.
"Where?!"

Zander hands me the card,
"In the bushes outside
the auditorium lobby."

"It's not roped off
from the fire?"

"Nah, they cleared it up
for tomorrow's concert."

I FOLD MY ARMS

Plop onto my bed.

Zander sits beside me.
"He still not letting you
go to it?"

I shake my head no.

"Maybe he's right.
Something weird
is going on.
It keeps finding a way
to involve you."

I hold
the three
mystery cards
in my hand.

INTERRUPTED

"Gonna grab
dinner with Nani,"
Dad calls from the hallway.

Zander quickly
stands up.

Dad peeks
into my room.

"We'll pick you up food
on the way back,"
says Dad.
He looks at Zander.
"You think you'll
still be here by then?"

"Um . . ."
Zander pauses.
He knows how
Dad feels about
boys being over
when he isn't around.

But . . . it's just Zander.

ZANDER STICKS HIS HANDS IN HIS POCKETS

He says,
"My mom didn't
want me out for long,"

Dad nods his head.
"Lots of weird stuff
happening lately."

Zander nods back.
"Lots."

No talking.

Only nodding.

I BREAK THE SILENCE

"I need to
work on my
art assignment
anyway.
I'll see you
Monday, Zander."

Zander waves bye.
"See ya."

Dad's eyes
follow Zander
as he walks
out of the room.

Dad's eyes
shift back to me.
He raises one eyebrow.

I shake my head and say,
"Door closed, please."

DAD BRINGS ME A TORTA

Nani only comes in
to tell me goodbye.
She winks to me
on her way out.

Dad walks her to her Jeep.

I'm nearly finished
eating by the time
he comes back inside.

"You know, I was thinking,"
Dad tells me.
"You really have
practiced a lot
for that concert."

I wait to take
my last bite.

Dad says,
"And it would be
a waste of money
to have bought you
that new piano.
Just to not let you
show off your talent."

I RUSH UP TO DAD

"You for real?"
I ask.

"Yup,"
Dad says.
"You can play at
tomorrow's concert."

I jump up
and down.
"Thank you!
Thank you!"

WE ALMOST HUG

Instead,
we pat
backs.

Hugging
each other
isn't something
we know
how to do.

Dad says,
"Promise me
you won't
hold back
tomorrow.
You'll leave it
all on the stage."

I nod,
"I promise."

BEFORE I GO TO MY ROOM

I tell Dad,
"For what
it's worth,
I like Nani."

Dad lets a grin slip out.
"I think I like her, too.
Is that something
you're cool with?"

I say,
"You're getting old.
It's about time
you found someone."

Dad rolls his eyes.

"So you know,"
Dad clears his throat.
"I think Zander
is a good kid."

I know
what he
means by
that.

I crinkle my nose.
"Ew, Zander is just a friend."

"Alright, alright."
Dad yawns as he
turns off the lights.
"I must've misread it."

LATE NIGHT SELF-PORTRAIT

I finally sketch
a version of me
that I don't hate.

I don't love it.
But I don't mind it, either.

With charcoal pencils,
I fill my features in.
From light, to dark.
From dark, to light.

Most other students
are using colors.

Black and white
suits me best.
This or that
is how I've always
seen myself.
In or out.
Hot or cold.
My brain only knows

extremes.

MY PHONE DINGS

A
text
message.

From

Gustavo.

Gustavo

Sup, stranger?

Me

ummm . . .Hi?

Gustavo

Surprised you're up this late.

Me

ummm . . . Hi?

Gustavo

Probably weren't expecting this, huh?

WHAT GUSTAVO TEXTS ME ABOUT

Gustavo
has been
thinking
about me
lately.

He's been wanting to
check how I'm doing.

To make sure
I'm okay
after everything
that's happened
this week.

Rey wouldn't
let him.

He's super jealous.

Gustavo couldn't
take it anymore.

That's why he
broke up with Rey
this morning.

Gustavo asks if
I'm free to hang
after tomorrow's concert.

GUSTAVO'S INVITATION

makes my
stomach stir.

I can't tell

if it's

butterflies

or

banshees.

ALL THE PAST TIMES

Gustavo made me feel good
become clear
in my mind.

As if all 40
of my *brujo* cards
are laid out before me.

A slideshow of
holding hands
between classes.

Matching outfits for
themed pep rallies.

Making out behind
the band hall.

Him whispering my name
to check if I was still awake
during phone calls at 2 a.m.

His black eyes reflecting
my hopeless teen smile
that doesn't know any better.

Then,
my heart reminds me
how our past was not
only perfect memories.

I quickly ignore the bad ones.

I TELL HIM YES

This answer feels

entirely right

and

entirely wrong

at the same time.

I WANT TO TEXT HIM ALL NIGHT

Instead,

Gustavo
stops
responding.

Five
minutes
go by.

Ten
minutes
go by.

I fidget
my legs.
Like they're
covered in ants.

WAITING FOR GUSTAVO TO TEXT BACK MAKES ME FEEL

Stupid.

Angry.

Anxious.

With my darkest
charcoal pencil,

I draw jagged lines
over my self-portrait.

From the center
of the face
to the edges
of the page.

Like

a

cracked

mirror.

I DOUBLE-TEXT GUSTAVO

Me
u there?

Then 41 minutes and 32 seconds later . . .

Gustavo
heading to bed. c u tomorrow.

Me
Ah, okay.

Glad we got to chat.

Goodnight, Tavo

I WAIT FOR A GOODNIGHT TEXT

It doesn't come.

I stay up

the whole
night.

Feeling

Hurt—
Because I
hate seeing
myself this way.

Helpless—
Because I
keep going
in circles.

Hopeless—
Because I
don't think
things will
be different
this time.

SATURDAY PERFECTION

I wake up early
to be first in line
at the barbershop.
Get the
cleanest cut
he's given
all year.

I skip lunch
to prepare for
the evening
band concert.

Clean shave.
Teeth whitener.
Moldable hair wax.
Concealer to
hide pimples.
Smoky black makeup
around my eyes.
Tiny star glitter, too.
Ironed gray slacks
and black button-up shirt.
Polished leather boots.
Rose gold bolo.
Sage cologne.

It takes hours
to perfect my look.

WINTER BAND CONCERT

I arrive at
the auditorium
one hour early.
Wait for Gustavo
in the student
drop-off area.

Zander arrives.
"Is that a new *zarape*?
I like the floral pattern.
And how it shimmers
in the light."

I tell him,
"Sorta. Dad got it for me
during junior high.
Finally doesn't look
like I'm wearing a *colcha*."

"Nah, it fits you perfectly."

"¿Neta?"

"Neta."

I smile widely.
More than usual.
I try to hide it
by looking down.

"What you so happy about, Ale?"

I HATE HOW WELL ZANDER KNOWS ME

"What?"
I giggle.
Straighten my face.

Zander squints.
"Something's
up with you."

"I don't
know what
you're talking
about."

Zander exhales loudly,
"Is this about
Gustavo and Rey
breaking up?"

I say nothing.

Blush.

Zander groans,
"Are you serious, Ale?"

I groan back.
"Zander."

"After all he
put you through?!"

"It's not that simple!"

"For everyone
on the outside
looking in?
Yeah.
It's pretty simple.
He's no good for you!"

I CHECK MY PHONE

Gustavo hasn't
texted me back
since this morning.
He was supposed
to meet me out here
before the concert.

Zander says,
"Ale. You deserve better."

I stuff my phone
into my pocket.

Look Zander
in the eye.

Think of all
the reasons
why he's wrong.

About how
I deserve better.

About how
Gustavo can't change.

Zander steps closer.

Softly, he says,
"Ale—"

DIRECTOR GUERRERO WALKS OUTSIDE

"Students, inside!
Time to warm up!"
She waves us in.

I
turn
my
back
to
Zander.

Leave
for the
auditorium

without him.

ONSTAGE

Section by section,
the musicians tune
their instruments.

As a band,
we practice scales. Chords.

At some point
during all that,
Gustavo hurries in.
Late.
He doesn't look
my way once.

A maroon hickey
peeks out from
beneath his shirt collar.

Convincing myself
he got it before last night
keeps me from
totally losing it.

My ears burn red.
Like chiles.

To keep my hands busy,
I shuffle my deck
of 40 cards.
Along with
the three cards
found this week.

EVERY SEAT IS FULL

Dad brought Nani.
She waves once I spot them.

The audience lighting dims.
The stage lights brighten. Like suns.

Everyone becomes quiet.

All the band kids
straighten their posture.

I shove my cards
into my back pocket.
Place my hands
over the piano keys.

Director Guerrero
raises her baton.
Waves her hands
to set the pace.
All the band kids
take a deep breath.

Director Guerrero
counts us in,
"Three, Two, One . . ."

BEFORE THE FIRST NOTE PLAYS

the stage shakes.

Like there's
an earthquake.

But we don't get
earthquakes in

Deep South Texas.

TIME PORTAL

People jump up
from their seats.
Screaming.
Dust glides down
from the rafters.

Above the band,
blue lightning flashes.
Over and over.
Like veins.
Like cracks.
The air splits apart.
Like curtains pulled open.

A tear in space and time.

Chilling wind
and cobalt fog
pour out of it.

Director Guerrero
leads everyone
off the stage.

I stand.

Cold.
Frozen.

Mesmerized
by the lightning storm
inside the time portal.

RATTLING SOUNDS

from inside
the time portal.

A rattlesnake
as wide as a car
slithers out of it.
Smooth as oil.
Midnight-blue scales.
Horns on its snout.
A bony, white rattle
at its end.

It crushes all the
folding chairs
on the stage.
Coils itself
into a ball.
Shakes its
rattle loudly.
Whips its
black tongue.
Lifts its head
into the air.

There's a long scar
across the bottom
of its mouth.

It hisses,
"Where . . . is . . . he?"

SOMETHING FAMILIAR

Zander reaches my side.
"Alejandro!"
he shouts.

The snake quickly
looks our way.
Its glowing
white eyes
look down at us.

Zander stands
in front of me.
Like a shield.

"Wait."
I place my hand
on Zander's shoulder.
"I don't think it
means to harm us."

"*Now* you choose
to be optimistic?!"
Zander huffs.

I walk ahead of Zander.
"There's something
familiar about it."

GUSTAVO FLEES

The snake watches
Gustavo run past me.
Gustavo leaps off the
ledge of the stage.
Ready to escape.

But the snake
catches him
midair with its tail.

Dozens of security officers
rush toward the stage.
Wands raised.

Before they can
attack the snake,
the snake breathes
out a snow blizzard.
It forms into
a solid wall.
A dome
over the
entire stage.

Gustavo, Zander, and I
are now
trapped
with the
time-traveling demon.

THE SNAKE SQUEEZES GUSTAVO

I shout at the snake,
"Let him go!"

"Let him go?!"
the snake roars.
"Never!
He is the reason
why I am here.
Why we are
the way
we are!"

I gasp.
"We?!"

The snake says,
"Yes, Alejandro. We."

Then he continues:
"I am you from the future."

THE SNAKE EXPLAINS

"Tonight after
the concert,
you'll hang out
with Gustavo.
You'll forgive him
for hurting you.
But he will soon
hurt you again.
And you will
forgive him again.
Over. And over.
An endless cycle.
One you can't break.
For years to come.
You will lose the
warmth inside you.
A little more
every time the
cycle repeats.
Until you become
consumed by bitterness.
And allow
Cold Magic
into your heart."

The snake says,
"In the future,
you time traveled
to the past.
Your mission was
to stop tonight's
concert from happening.
That way,
you and Gustavo
would never
get back together.
Your first attempt—
turning a *chicharra*
into a giant that
destroyed the piano.
Your second attempt—
setting the auditorium on fire.
No matter what you did,
you failed your mission.
The concert still
took place.
And the futures
you returned to
were worse and
worse each time.
Cold Magic
froze your heart.
Turned you into
the beast you see
before you now."

The snake says,
"We must
get rid of
Gustavo.
Send him to
another era
entirely.
Before
we allow
him to
ruin
our
future."

The snake
dangles Gustavo
over the
time portal.

"Don't!"
Gustavo begs.
"Please!
I'm sorry!"

SEEING GUSTAVO BEG AND CRY

It brings a
sparkle to
my eye.

It does the same
for the snake.
Me from the future.
The version of me
that refuses
to be healed.

> "Ale! No!"
> Zander shouts.
> "You need to forgive him!"

I blink rapidly.
As if waking up.

I tell Zander,
"No."

JUST LIKE EVERYONE ALWAYS DOES

"You have to
forgive him!"
Zander shakes me.
Like a doll.

"No!"
I push Zander away.
Point at Gustavo.
"No matter what,
you're going to
break my heart!"

I begin to sob.

The harder I do,
the larger the
snake becomes.

I yell,
"No matter what I do
to show my love,
you're going to abandon me.
Just like everyone does!
Just like everyone always does!"

I LOOK INTO THE TIME PORTAL

Visions from
different eras appear.
Dinosaurs roaming.
Pyramids. Castles.
Rocket ships blasting off
into space.

I see Dad's bedroom.
Back when I still
called him *Tío* Jorge.
There's shouting
behind the closed
bedroom door.
Shaking walls.
Shattering glass.

There's a child
hiding under a blanket.
Trembling. Ears covered.
Me at five years old.

I want to hug him.

Tell him it's
going to be okay.

But I wonder if I'd be lying.
Because look at all
his future holds.

EVERYTHING MOVES SLOWLY

Zander grabs my shoulders.
Faces me away
from the time portal.
Shouts my name over. And over.

Behind him, I see Dad.
Pounding his fists
against the ice wall.
Desperate to get in.
Where he can protect me.

People who love me most.
I always seem to
keep them on the outside.
I'm so scared that one day
their love for me will run out.
And then they'll walk away.

Zander looks me in the eye.
"So many of us care about you, Ale.
We aren't going to abandon you."

I see my reflection in Zander's eyes.
See myself the way he sees me.
The version of me that
can still change the future.
Be better than my father was.
Not give in to my coldest desires.
Learn how to let go.

THE SOLUTION

I hold my breath.
Drown out the shouts.
The rattling.
The thunder.
Force time
to stand still
in my mind.

I tell Zander,
"Forgiving him
isn't the solution."

As I speak, the snake
slowly begins to shrink.

"Forgiveness is a decision
I'll have to make every day
for the rest of my life,"
I say.
"The solution is letting him go."

I quickly reach into my pocket.
Pull out the three cards that
belonged to versions of me
from the future.
Throw them to the floor.

A cracked mirror.

A snake swallowing its tail.

A broken clock.

LETTING GO

"I forgive you, Gustavo,"
I whisper.
"And I let you go.
I will never again
hold on to what harms me."

"He must pay!"
the snake roars.

The snake loosens
its grip on Gustavo.

Gustavo falls

toward

the

time

portal.

A BETTER FUTURE

The snake,
ice dome,
three cards,
and time portal
begin to flash rapidly.
Like lightning and static.

I whisper
one last time,
"I let you go, Gustavo."

THE CARDS CHANGE

The cracked mirror
becomes whole.

The snake undoes itself
and slithers away.

The clock begins ticking
once more.

Less than a second
before Gustavo falls
into the time portal,

the ice dome,
snake,
three cards,
and time portal
vanish in a flash
of lightning.

Gustavo

crashes

onto

the

floor

instead.

DAD RUSHES ONTO THE STAGE

"Are you okay?!"
He wraps me in a hug.

"I'm going to be okay,"
I say.
I allow
myself
to be held.
"I'm safe now."

Zander and Nani join us.
They wrap their arms
around me, too.

GUSTAVO LIMPS OVER

"Ale,"
Gustavo says.
"I'm sorry.
We should talk.
About everything."

"No,"
I tell him.
Surrounded
by my family.

"Goodbye, Gustavo."

NEW YEAR'S EVE

Our home is filled
with Dad and Nani's friends.

Party hats. Ribbons.
Colorful sparklers.
Buckets of tamales.

Dad gathers us around a curtain
pinned over the wall.

He removes the
curtain and shouts,
"Ta-da!"

It's my self-portrait
for Mrs. De Luna's class.
I turned the jagged lines
I drew out of frustration
into lines for a color wheel.
Each of the six colors
represents my emotions.

Yellow, joyful.
Blue, sad.

All of my emotions
are equally valid. And magical.
They make up who I am as a person.
As a *brujo*.

Everyone *oohs* and *aahs*
at the sight of my truest form.

JUST BEFORE MIDNIGHT

Zander shows up.

"Did I miss
the big reveal?"
Zander smiles.

"Like you haven't seen it
a dozen times already,"
I say.

Zander follows me
into the kitchen.

"One minute left!"
Dad announces
from the
living room.

That's where
everyone's
gathered.

"Make sure you have
someone to kiss!"
Nani laughs.

"Or bite!"
Dad teases her.

JUST US TWO

"You think the
stroke of midnight
actually changes anything?"
I lean against the counter.
"Or is it just some
fireworks industry scam?"

"A lot can change in one second."
Zander leans beside me.
"Entire timelines, in fact.
Or did you already forget
demon-snake-you from the future?"

I roll my eyes. Smirk.

Zander's smile
looks like
a squiggly line.

I can tell
something's
on his mind.

"What is it?"
I ask.

Zander reaches

into his pocket.

ELEVEN . . . TEN . . .

Zander pulls
his balled fist
out of his pocket.

He holds it
out to me.

His fingers
peel back.
Like a
blooming
flower.

In his palm is

an origami penguin.

Folded out of
rose gold foil.

Like the one
that was left

on my piano
in the band hall.

NINE . . . EIGHT . . .

Our eyes lock.

I suddenly
see Zander
in a different light.

One I could never
see before.

Not without
first learning
that I deserve
to be loved.

SEVEN . . . SIX . . .

I take the
origami penguin

into my hand.

Hold it
against
my racing

heart.

FIVE . . . FOUR . . .

Zander

leans

toward

me.

THREE . . . TWO . . .

I lean

toward

Zander.

ONE . . .

We

close

our eyes.

WANT TO KEEP READING?

If you liked this book, check out another book from West 44 Books:

SAMSON & DOMINGO

BY GUME LAUREL III

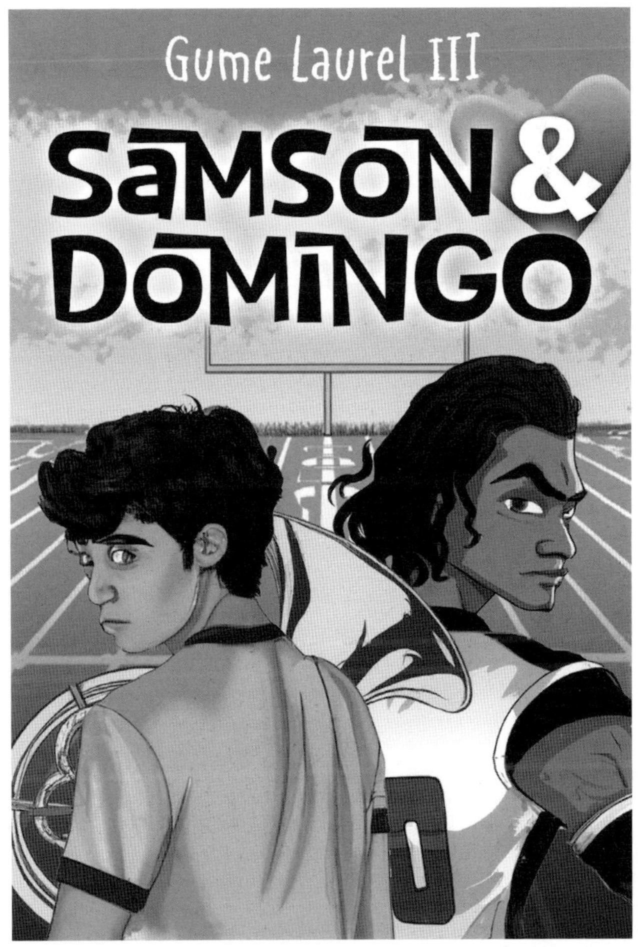

ISBN: 9781978597099

Samson's Hair

is too pretty for a jock's head.

Equal parts dark cocoa and milky smooth.

Runs longer than any high school math class.

I have no clue how he fits it all into

his football helmet for Friday Night Lights.

Samson Montaña &
Domingo Paloma

We are the definition of star-crossed lovers.

Pop vs. Indie

Meathead vs. Band geek

Attending rival high schools
in the same city

widens the divide.

But, it doesn't keep us from
texting each other around the clock.

Early Afternoon

Samson

Happy two-month anniversary since we first met, Domingo.

Me

You're such a simp lol.

Samson

Guess you don't want your gift then.

Me

Happy two-month anniversary, Samson!

Waltzing into the Living Room

I wear a lavender, fitted polo.
Warm rosewood cologne on my collar.
It trails into the air around me. Like butterflies.

My older brother, Pablo,
sits on the couch.

I plop down beside him. Lace up my
black Converse.

"Again, Domingo? You're going somewhere with
Man Bun?"
Pablo scrolls on his phone.

NO PLACE
for
FAIRY TALES

DANDELION
TRAVELS

REACHING
FOR
VENUS
MAIJA BARNETT

ONLY
PIECES
edd tello

COUNTDOWN TO MIDNIGHT

"Fifteen seconds!"
Dad shouts.

Everyone
in the
living room
begins to
count
down.

ABOUT THE AUTHOR

Gume is a Texan, native to the Rio Grande Valley on the southernmost border. For the past decade, he has dedicated himself to crafting literary works that promote inclusion and showcase diverse characters with intersectional identities. The bulk of Gume's writings are focused on underrepresented groups, especially those from the communities he is a part of: Latine and queer. Gume's first verse novel, *Samson & Domingo*, was published by West 44 Books in Spring of 2024. When Gume isn't writing, he can be found getting lost on a hiking trail with his dogs Blu and Mouse. For more info on what he's up to, check out GumeLaurel.com and @TX.Author